The Goodnight Train Rolls On!

To the family poet, my grandfather Abe Sobel.
—J. S.

This book is dedicated to Jake.
We're pretty sure he's herding naughty sheep
in Dreamland as we roll on.
—L. H. B.

hmhco.com

The illustrations in this book were done in acrylic paints with fabric and paper collage.
The display lettering was created by Laura Huliska-Beith.
The text type was set in Pink Martini.

Library of Congress Cataloging-in-Publication Data is on file.
ISBN: 978-1-328-50019-9

Manufactured in China
SCP 10 9 8 7 6 5 4 3 2 1
4500710935

The Goodnight Train Rolls On!

June Sobel

Illustrated by Laura Huliska-Beith

Houghton Mifflin Harcourt

Boston   New York

See you in the MORNING!

DREAM DUST
DEPOT

FREE
REFILLS

Stars are twinkling. Moon shines bright.
The Goodnight Train chugs through the night.

Dream dust lands on sleepy heads.
The porter smiles and fluffs the beds.

Chugga! Chugga!
Shhhhhhh! Shhhhhhh!

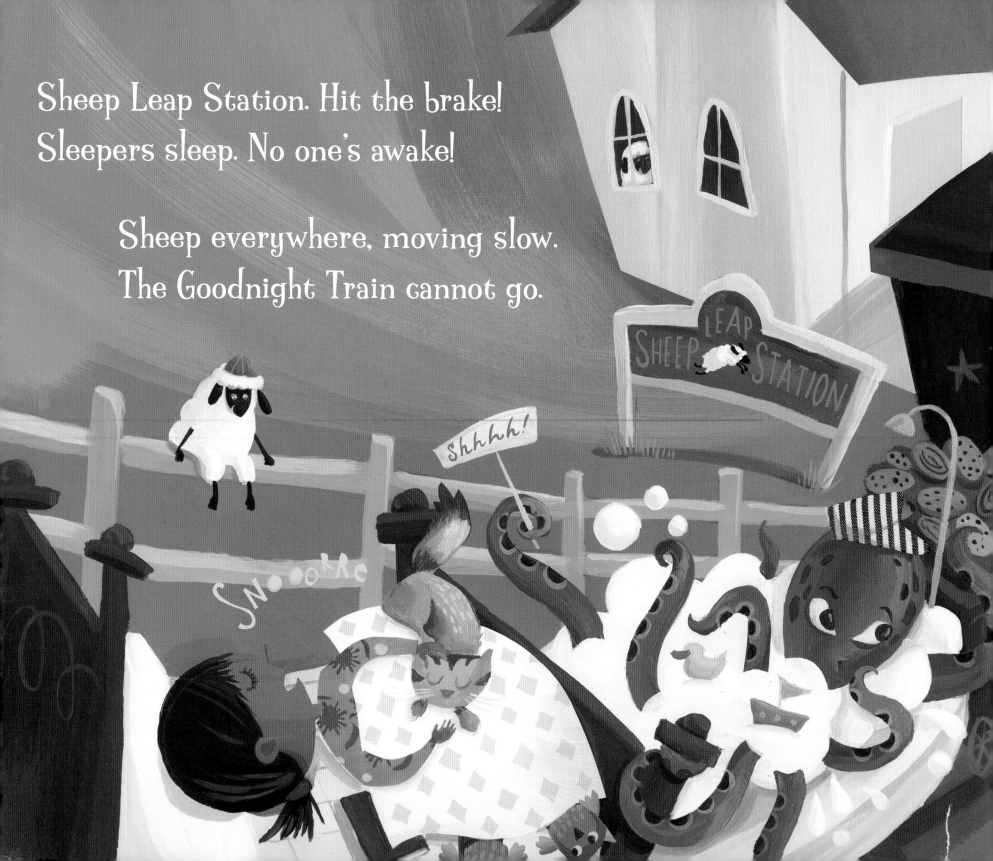

Sheep Leap Station. Hit the brake!
Sleepers sleep. No one's awake!

Sheep everywhere, moving slow.
The Goodnight Train cannot go.

They push and shove and rock the train.

Baahh! Baahh! Baahh!

the sheep complain.

Sleepers toss and turn their heads, wiggling, jiggling in their beds.

The engineer has a great idea!
Count the sheep till the track is clear.

Over the fence, they start to leap
until everyone is fast asleep!

Chugga! Chugga!
Shhhhhhh!
Shhhhhhh!

The Goodnight Train slips and slides
on Midnight Mountain's steep hillside.

Just before they reach the top,
the engine makes a sudden stop.

At the peak, the moonlight's bright,
shining like the sun at night!

Sleepers cover up their heads,
wiggling, jiggling in their beds.

Umbrellas open left and right.
Back to sleep. No more light.

Clouds blow in. The night turns gray.
The Goodnight Train is on its way!

Chugga! Chugga!

Shhhhhh!
Shhhhhh!

Down Midnight Mountain, race along
until something seems very wrong!

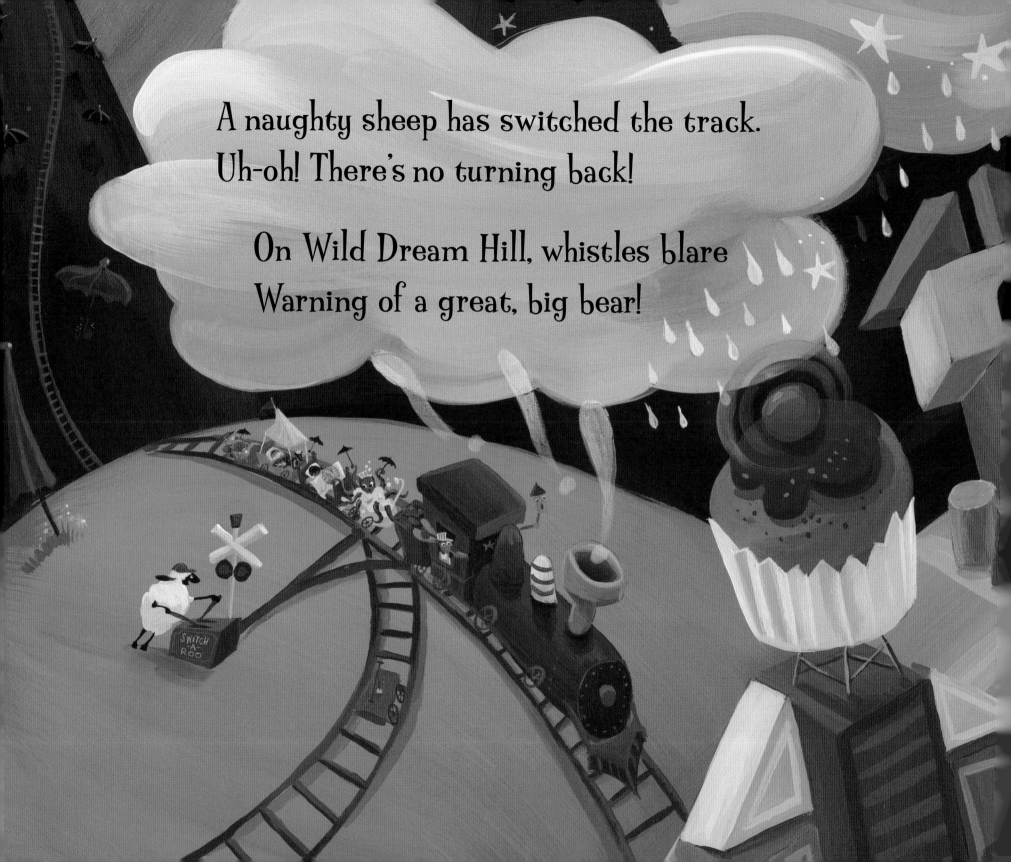

A naughty sheep has switched the track.
Uh-oh! There's no turning back!

On Wild Dream Hill, whistles blare
Warning of a great, big bear!

Sleepers toss and turn their heads,
wiggling, jiggling in their beds.

Pillow fight! Bear doesn't care.
Catching each one in the air!

Train whistle toots a brand new tune,
a lullaby of stars and moon!

Big teddy sways and twirls around
and lands fast asleep on the ground!

The engine puffs up smoke and steam.
The sleepers smile and dream a dream.

The Goodnight Train's work is done.
Soon moon and stars will fade to sun.

Chugga! Chugga!
Shhhhhhh! Shhhhhhh!

Good night, train.

Good night.

FREE
REFILLS